THIS WALKER BOOK BELONGS TO:

_____

_____

_____

_____

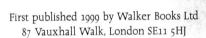

For Noreen Amis
and Caroline Butler,
and for Amelia
with thanks.

First published 1999 by Walker Books Ltd
87 Vauxhall Walk, London SE11 5HJ

This edition published 2000

2 4 6 8 10 9 7 5 3 1

© 1999 Kathy Henderson

This book has been typeset in Opti Cather.

Printed in Hong Kong

British Library Cataloguing in Publication Data
A catalogue record for this book is
available from the British Library.

ISBN 0-7445-7827-2

KATHY HENDERSON

The Storm

WALKER BOOKS

AND SUBSIDIARIES

LONDON • BOSTON • SYDNEY

Jim stood on the high grass bank
and stretched out his arms
like the sails of the windmill.

"All this is mine!"
he shouted at the wind.

Winter was nearly over.
The tide came in and the tide went out.

The beaches were empty and
flocks of geese gathered on the marshes.

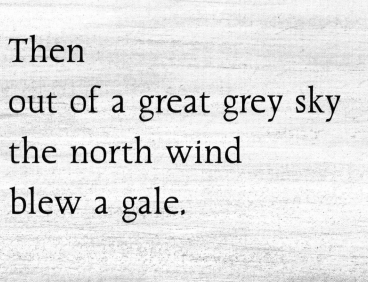

Then
out of a great grey sky
the north wind
blew a gale.

All night long the wind raged.
It stirred up the sea, bent trees,
crashed tiles, smashed flowerpots,

rattled at the doors and windows
and tore through the dreams
of people sleeping.

The village sirens
wailed a flood warning.
Wake up!

Jim stumbled to the window
and looked out past the gate
and the road
and over the marsh
to the straight line
where the beach met the sky
just getting light.

What was that?
A splash of white.
Gone now.
No, It can't have been,
Yes! There's another
and another
bigger white wave
breaking over
the top of the beach
and pouring down
on to the land.

"Mum! Mum!
The sea! It's coming!"

Jim and his mother
ran in the dawn,
   climbed the high grass bank
to try and see.
   Up and up,
until the wind slapped their faces
and knocked them back.
   One more step to
      be able to look over...

But there was no over! The marsh had gone.
The windmill was surrounded and
in the distance where the beach had been

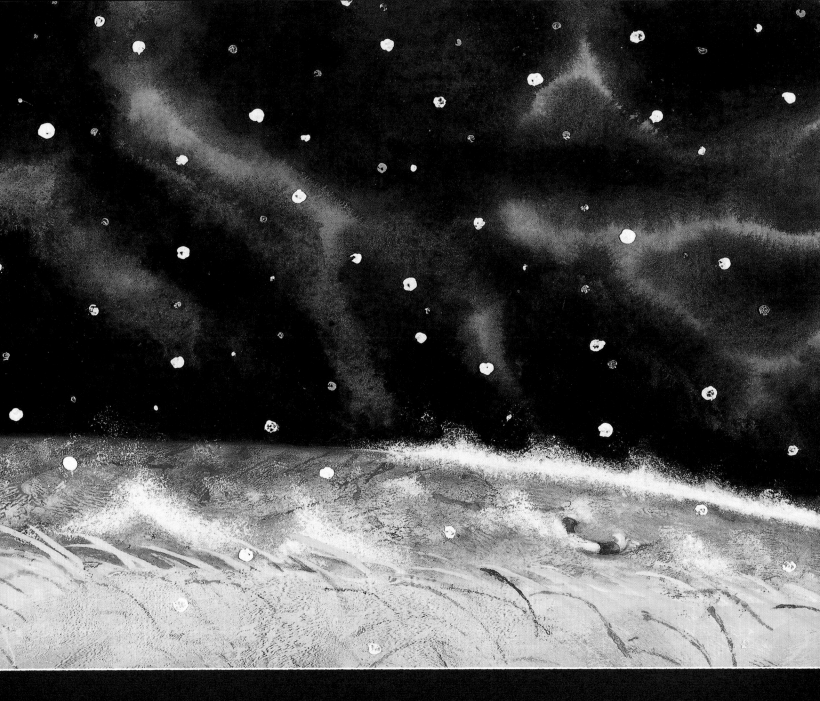

there was just a line of wild waves pounding.
"All this is mine!" roared the wind
and the sky hurled hail.

They ran for home,
stacked sandbags against the doors
and struggled up the hill
to Grandma's house.

"What shall we do
if the sea comes in?
Where shall we
go then?" asked Jim.

"Come in. Get warm.
You're safe up here.
The sea may rage
but the land is strong.
Come and we'll wait
for the tide to turn."

The wind rattled.
The radio chattered.
The clock in the hall ticked
as if nothing was the matter.

Ten past seven.
They sat and waited.
Half past seven was
crawling towards eight
when Jim called out,
"Oh look, Mum, look!
It's all right.
The water's going down!"

The storm had passed. Winter was nearly over.
Jim stood on the beach in the sun and
stretched out his arms
like the sails of
the windmill.

"All this is yours," he whispered to the wind
and the sea lapped against the sand
quiet as a lamb.

The Storm

KATHY HENDERSON'S personal experience of a stormy night in winter was her inspiration for *The Storm*. She says, "I was staying with friends on the north Norfolk coast, right beside the marshes that run out to the shingle bank and the sea. As I slept, a strange, wailing noise crept into my dreams and wouldn't stop. I woke up. It was dark. The wailing sound from my dreams continued. It was the flood warning. I went to the window and in the first grey light of the dawn saw the waves breaking through the shingle bank and the water spreading out towards us. That's where this story began."

Kathy Henderson has written many children's books, including
15 Ways to Go to Bed (shortlisted for the Smarties Book Prize);
In the Middle of the Night; *The Little Boat* (Winner of the Kurt Maschler Award and shortlisted for the Smarties Book Prize); *A Year in the City* (Winner of the 'Primary English' Book Award) and *The Baby Dances*.
The Storm has been shortlisted for the 2000 Kate Greenaway Medal.
Kathy Henderson has three children and lives in London.

ISBN 0-7445-5253-2 (pb)

ISBN 0-7445-3143-8 (pb)

ISBN 0-7445-6042-X (pb)

ISBN 0-7445-6360-7 (pb)